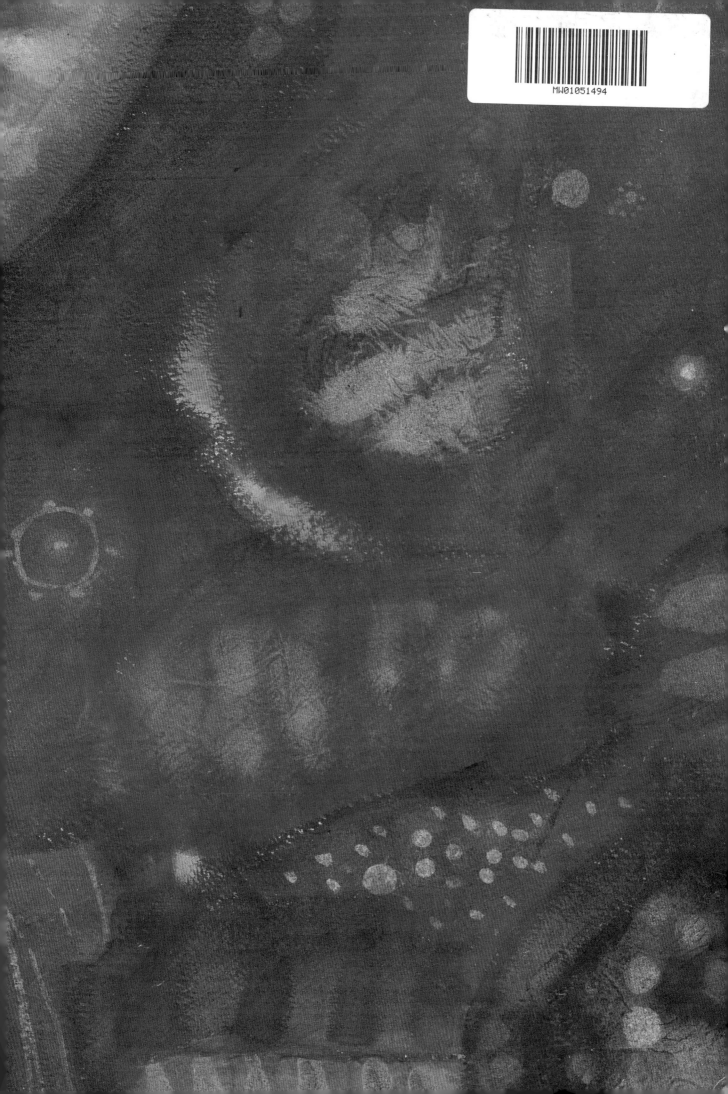

First published in Belgium and Holland by Clavis Uitgeverij, Hasselt – Amsterdam, 2010
Copyright © 2010, Clavis Uitgeverij

English translation from the Dutch by Clavis Publishing Inc. New York
Copyright © 2011 for the English language edition: Clavis Publishing Inc. New York

Visit us on the web at www.clavisbooks.com

Thankyouplease written by Pierre Winters and illustrated by Barbara Ortelli
Original title: *Dankjewelalsjeblieft*
Translated from the Dutch by Clavis Publishing

ISBN 978-1-60537-099-6

This book was printed in March 2011 at Proost,
Everdongenlaan 23, B-2300 Turnhout, Belgium

First Edition
10 9 8 7 6 5 4 3 2 1

Thankyou please

Pierre Winters & Barbara Ortelli

Clavis

NEW YORK

Nina is six years old and she wears her hair in braids.

Nina is not very tall and she is not very strong.

Nina has a big mouth. She is often grumpy and talks back. That's when she says, "NO! NO! NO!"

That's also when she says "I WILL NOT!" and "I DON'T CARE!"

Mommy tries to teach her daughter good manners. She doesn't like it when Nina acts so grumpy and rude.

"That's not nice, Nina," Mommy will say. "If you would be a bit more polite, people would see how sweet you can be and want to play with you."

But today Nina is in a bad mood and she shakes her head.

"No! I don't care! I want candy now!" she howls.

Mommy suggests that Nina go outside to calm down. Nina storms into the garden.

She scolds her dog, Hugo, who whines and curls up in a ball.

Then Nina puts on her flowerpot helmet.
She is a knight – a brave, tough knight, not afraid of
anybody.

Nina yawns. Being grumpy and rude is tiring.
She yawns again.

"Hey, Nina, come here!"

Who is calling her? Where is the voice coming
from? Nina looks around.

"Nina!" Someone calls again.

Nina sees a hole in one of the tree trunks – a hole that she's not noticed before! Curiously she walks towards it. She peeks inside.

A circus!

A blue elephant is balancing on a ball. A cat is balancing a bucket above its head.

Nina claps her hands in delight. Then she sees little Hugo riding a big bicycle! And, boy, is he good!

"Welcome to the circus," the elephant says solemnly. "Would you like to join us?"

Nina nods.

"Then I will introduce you to our Ringmaster. Come in and wait right here, please."

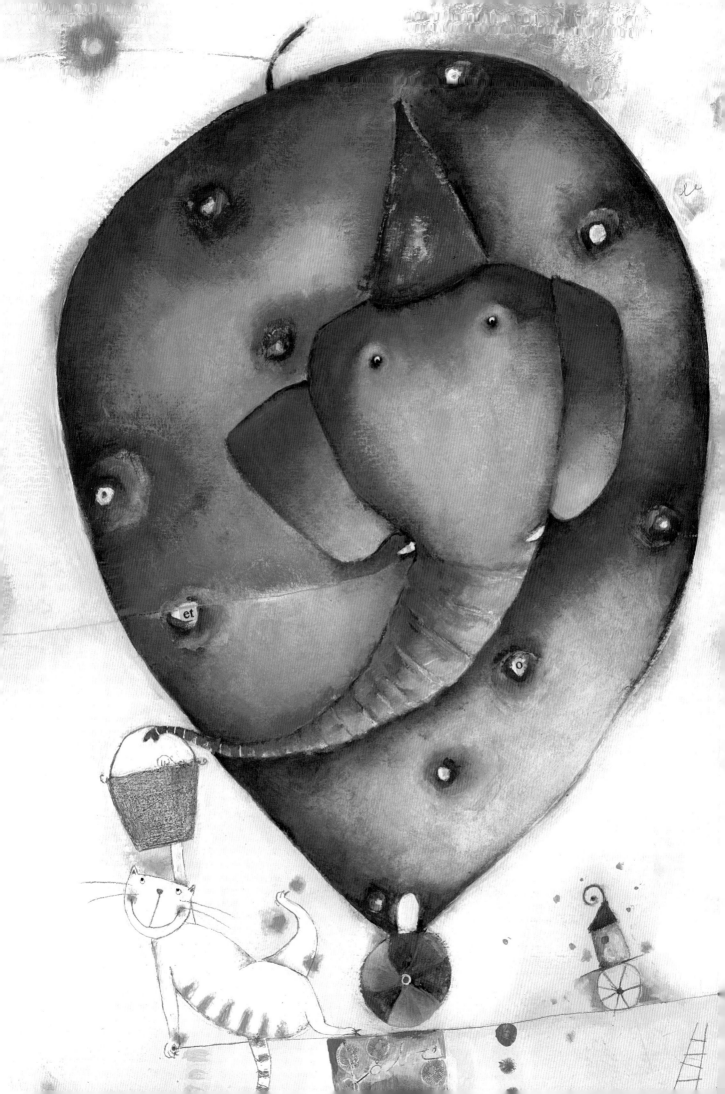

"Hello, Nina," the Ringmaster says. "My name is Thankyouplease. This is the Circus of Good Manners. We practice tricks and we practice good manners. You would like to join us, am I right? If so, welcome to the show! Thankyouplease!"

Nina cannot speak. Before she can blink, she is following Thankyouplease inside the circus tent.

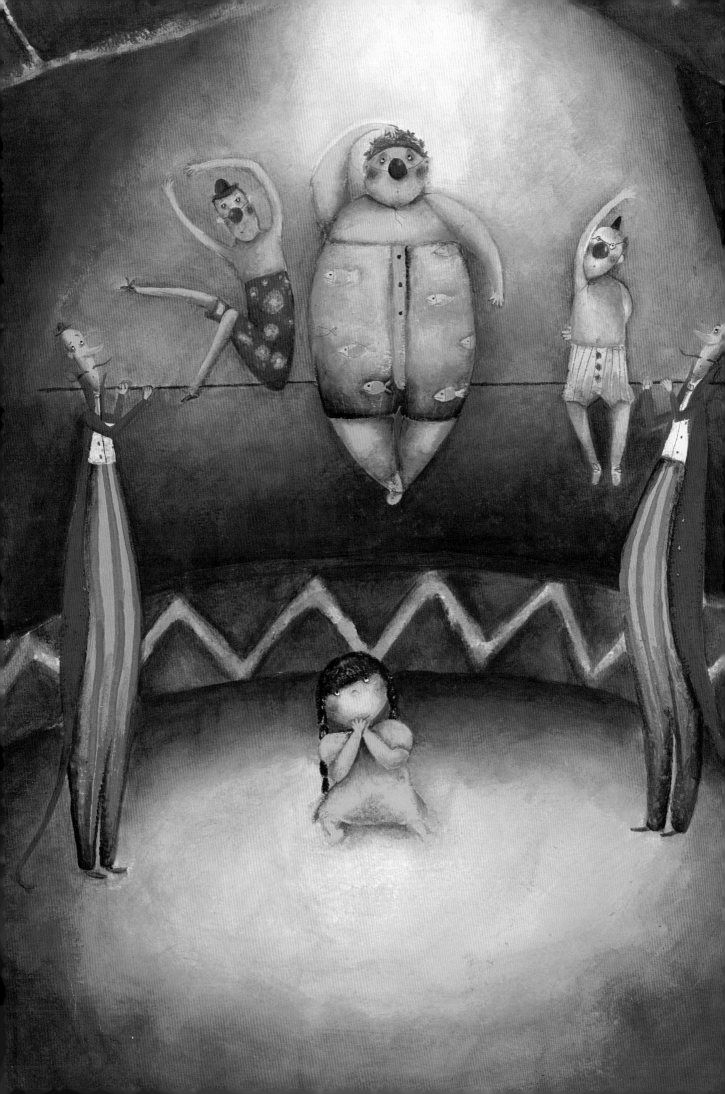

In the ring two slim giants are balancing a wooden beam
on their shoulders. Three men are standing on the beam.
   "Please show Nina your tricks, gentlemen,"
the Ringmaster says.
      The men on the beam turn somersaults. One says,
"Good morning!" Another says, "Good afternoon!"
And the third one says, "Good night!"
      The men invite Nina to balance on the beam.
She turns somersaults with them and chants,
   "Good morning! Good afternoon!
   Good night!"
      "That is the very nicest way to greet
people," explains the Ringmaster.

Next to the ring an old lady is giving away cotton candy. People are waiting patiently in line. They don't push. They don't pull. And when they get their cotton candy, they say, "Thank you!"

Nina wants cotton candy very much. But the only way she can get some is to join the end of the long, long line. She waits. When it is finally her turn, she is so happy to finally have the candy, she says, "Thank you!" to the old lady.

"It's always polite to say 'Thank you' when something is given to you," the Ringmaster explains.

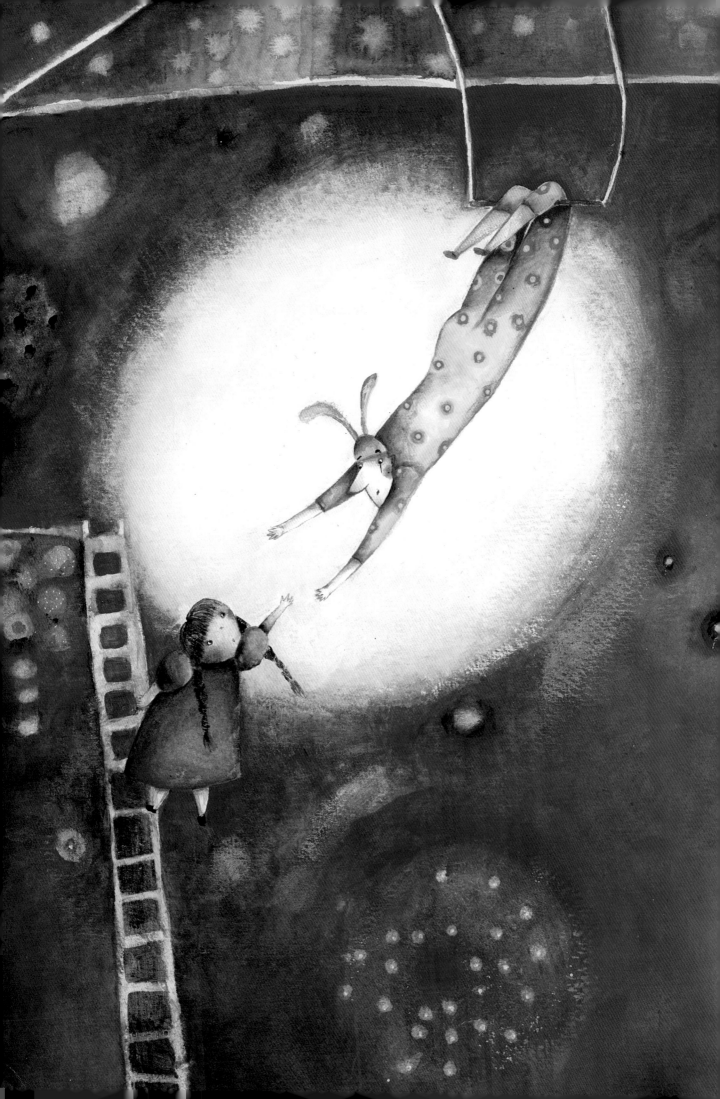

Way up at the ridge of the tent, trapeze artists are practicing. They look like they're flying! Nina wants to fly too! Quickly she climbs to the top of a tall, skinny ladder.

"If you want to join in, you have to pay attention to what everyone else is doing," one of the acrobats says. "It's only by helping each other that we won't fall."

Nina nods and swings herself on a trapeze. *Oh, how scary!* Then she lets go and she is flying! Before she can fall, she is caught by two strong arms.

"There you go," says the acrobat, who sets her back down.

"Thank you," Nina says. And she means it.

Then it is her turn to help catch one of the acrobats, who thanks her.

"You are welcome," Nina says instantly.

Back on the ground, Nina sees a clown on a funny bicycle.

"I want to ride that!" Nina yells and she tries to push the clown. He does not fall, but bends at his waist, rights himself, and goes on riding.

"Hey, let me ride it!" Nina whines.

The clown seems not to hear her. The Ringmaster whispers something in her ear. Nina blushes and says, "Clown, may I please have a turn riding the bicycle?"

The clown jumps from the bicycle and bows.

"There you go, Nina. All you had to do was say 'Please' and wait your turn."

"Nina! It's time for dinner!"

Nina wakes up in the grass next to the tree.

"Where have you been all this time?" Mommy asks.

"At the circus of Thankyouplease! Oh, Mommy, it was wonderful!"

"I am sure it was," Mommy says. "Shall we have our dinner?"

"Oh, yes, Mommy, please. I am sure that you've prepared a delicious dinner."

Mommy looks at her daughter curiously.

"Shall I set the table, Mommy?" Nina asks.

"Yes, thank you, that would be lovely," Mommy answers, shaking her head in wonder.

After dinner, Nina thanks her mother, excuses herself and goes to her room with Hugo.

"You are a sweet dog," she says, patting his head. "And I'm sorry I scolded you before."

Hugo wags his tail and jumps in Nina's lap.

"Come on, Hugo! I want to teach you some tricks that are just as easy and fun as saying 'Thank you' and 'Please'."